CATNIP BOOKS
Published by Catnip Publishing Ltd.
320 City Road
London EC1V 2NZ

This edition published 2019
1 3 5 7 9 8 6 4 2

Text copyright © Pete Johnson 2019
Illustrations copyright © Mike Phillips 2019

A CIP catalogue record of this book is available from the British Library.

ISBN 978-1-910-61121-0

www.catnippublishing.co.uk

Printed and bound by CPI Group (UK) Ltd, Croydon CR0 4YY

WEREWOLF BROTHER

Pete Johnson

Illustrated by
Mike Phillips

Contents

1

Halloween

'No, Harry,' I cried. 'You can't have a werewolf for Halloween.'

'But, Jamie!' shouted Harry. 'Tomorrow night we'll be in our scary masks telling horror stories. And then we'll hear a werewolf howling . . . It will be SOOOO spooky.'

I hesitated.

'And I'll only wish for the teeniest, weeniest, titchiest werewolf,' Harry continued. 'And a really happy one too. He'll only *sound* fang-drippingly fierce and bloodthirsty. Go on, Jamie. I'll never ask you for anything else – EVER!'

It did sound totally fantastic. Our very own werewolf – on Halloween night. Could life get any better?

By the way, I have an incredible secret. I've got a cape that makes wishes come true.

I found it one day, high in the branches of a tree. It's dark blue with gold stars around the sides. And the brightest number

seven you've ever seen, just inside the collar. When you sprinkle it with water, it transforms into a MAGIC CAPE.

Recently, however, we've made so many wishes that we've practically used up all of its magic. I gazed at it lying on my bed. You could hardly see any of the gold stars, they were so faded.

'My cape needs a holiday from magic,' I said.

'No it doesn't.' Harry likes to argue about everything.

'Yes it does. You know what happened yesterday.'

Yesterday, Harry and I wished for something really simple. A giant ice cream. And we got our wish. It was a chocolate ice cream too – my favourite.

But before we could take one lick, the ice cream vanished and squirming about in my hand instead was a truly enormous brown spider, with a zillion legs. It leapt off my hand and started scuttling around my bedroom. It took absolutely ages to wish it away again.

'Right now, my cape is not working properly,' I explained. 'So we could wish for a happy werewolf but get something completely different, like a really terrifying werewolf. Imagine that, Harry.'

'Okay. All right then,' sighed Harry. But then, quick as a flash, he sprang forward and snatched my cape from the bed.

'Hey!' I yelled.

But he was already off, diving down the stairs. I raced after him. Harry is my

younger brother but, unfortunately, he's taller than me – and a much faster runner as well.

'Stop, thief!' I shouted at the top of my lungs.

Aunt Nora came rushing out of the kitchen. 'Boys, boys, stop this at once!' she cried.

Mum and Dad are away at a conference in America. Aunt Nora is looking after us. She's actually my mum's aunt, so she's very old indeed. She's normally so twinkly and jolly, but right now she looked a little bit cross.

'What a naughty carry-on,' she said.

Harry and I stopped charging about and stood glaring at each other.

'Now, boys, tell me what's wrong,' she said.

'Harry stole my cape,' I said.

'No, I didn't,' protested Harry. 'I borrowed it. And Jamie should share his things, shouldn't he, Aunt Nora?'

'Well, yes, he should . . .' she began.

'And I'll give it back soon,' Harry said eagerly.

'But he just grabbed it, without even asking me,' I protested.

'Oh dear,' said Aunt Nora. 'What a to-do.

But if you can't settle it nicely, you leave me no choice — I'll just have to cancel your Halloween party tomorrow.'

A look of horror shot across both our faces. Harry, very reluctantly, gave me back my cape.

'That's much better,' smiled Aunt Nora. 'You're both really such good boys. And I'm sure Jamie will let you play with his cape later, Harry.'

'I'm sure I won't,' I muttered. But at that moment the doorbell rang. It was Reema, holding a giant pumpkin.

'That looks absolutely splendid, Reema, dear,' said Aunt Nora. 'And I expect you want to take it over to your Halloween hideaway, which you have all decorated so charmingly.'

So Reema and I set off for the Halloween hideaway, which was right at the end of the garden. Harry was still sulking over the cape, so he didn't come with us.

Reema is my very best friend and the only other person who knows I have a magic cape. I quickly told her what had just happened.

'Don't worry, we can still have a great Halloween without any magic,' said Reema, and she patted my cape. 'The poor thing looks so tired and worn out.'

We reached what used to be an old garden shed, but was now transformed into our Halloween hideaway. We glanced round proudly at all our decorations – at the fake cobwebs and glow-in-the-dark window stickers. We positioned Reema's pumpkin on a small table, in pride of place.

'Look at this room!' cried Reema. 'It's waiting so impatiently for Halloween.'

'We're the impatient ones.' I grinned.

'By the way,' said Reema, 'I hope you don't mind, but I've asked Oscar to join us tomorrow.'

That was a shock. 'Do you mean Pongy?'

'Oh no, don't call him that.'

'Everyone else does,' I said.

Pongy is a new boy at our school. He's very small and very thin, with a really posh voice. His first lesson with us was PE. He walked into the boys' changing rooms and announced, 'It's a bit pongy in here.' After that 'Pongy' became his nickname. Every time someone calls him that he goes bright red. So of course people call him that ALL THE TIME!

'But why have you invited Pongy?' I asked.

'Because I think you're all very mean to . . . Oscar. And no one should be on their own at Halloween.'

'O-kay,' I said doubtfully. 'Anyway, I bet he won't turn up.'

'We'll see.' Reema smiled confidently. 'So, you think Harry will still try to use your cape?'

'Of course he will,' I replied. 'That's why I'm going to hide it from him in an ancient, battered case under my bed. It's where I keep my old comics.'

'Poor cape, having to be kept in a musty old case,' said Reema.

'It'll only be until tomorrow night,' I replied. 'And can you imagine the trouble if Harry wished for a werewolf and the magic went wrong?'

Reema shuddered. 'We certainly don't want that to happen,' she agreed.

2

A Face at the Window

It was Halloween night at last. I put on my monster mask. It had horrible bulging eyes and huge sharp teeth.

Soon Reema would arrive and it would be time for Halloween to really begin. But first I wanted to check on my magic cape. I dived under my bed and brought out the battered old case. Hidden under a pile of comics, as well as some of my smelliest, stinkiest socks, should have been my cape . . .

Yes, there it was! I had hoped the stars on it might have started to look a bit brighter, but they were just as faded as before.

Suddenly, my blood turned to ice. Had my cape been moved? Harry couldn't possibly have found it there. He couldn't have. *Could he?*

'WHOOOOOOOOO . . .' A very loud howling noise right outside my door made me jump.

Harry bounded in. He was wearing an incredibly hairy werewolf mask and claws, so his hands were sprouting hair too. He laughed excitedly at me. 'Ha ha. I scared you!' He had stopped sulking and now seemed very, very cheerful.

I stared at him most suspiciously. Why was he in such a good mood? Could he really have discovered my cape's secret hiding place? I was becoming more and more worried.

Suddenly, Aunt Nora appeared in the doorway. 'Well, I'm not taking another step nearer, you are both far too frightening,' she said.

At once Harry jumped about going 'WHOOOOOOOOO' again.

'Now I have left some treats in your hideaway,' Aunt Nora began.

'Your food is awesome and I'm starving,' shouted Harry. And he was off, thudding down the stairs. I followed him quickly.

'No need to rush, boys, you have plenty of time,' Aunt Nora called after us. 'I'll be along to see you all later.'

Harry sped down to the shed – he really was an incredibly fast runner.

I noticed there was a full moon lighting up the whole garden, making it look so mysterious and eerie. By the time I reached our Halloween hideaway, Harry was already stretched out on the big black swivel chair donated by Dad. We also had a sofa but it was very lumpy.

'I've got the best chair,' whooped Harry, swinging round and round on it.

'You'll have to let everyone else have a turn on the comfortable chair,' I said.

'No I won't, I'll sit here all night,' said Harry, whirling round again while snatching up one of Aunt Nora's home-made bat biscuits.

'Don't eat it yet,' I said. 'Wait for everyone else to get here first.'

'Stop telling me what to do,' said Harry, whirling round even faster and pushing the entire biscuit into his mouth. He immediately started coughing and spraying bits everywhere.

'Harry, please calm down,' I said. But Harry let out a giant burp.

'You are so gross,' I said. 'And messy and disgusting.'

Harry stuck his tongue out at me, which was now completely covered in crumbs.

'Harry . . .' I began. Then I froze. We both did.

We were not alone.

A figure was standing completely still in the doorway. It was dressed all in black

except for a truly horrible yellow pumpkin face.

Then the figure spoke. 'I can't wear this mask for long – it's too tight,' it said.

It was Reema.

'Wow, Reema!' I cried. 'Your mask is fantastic. Where did you get it?'

'I borrowed it from my cousin, which is why it doesn't fit very well,' she explained.

'And that black robe . . . ? I asked.

'That was Mum's idea,' she said.

'Well, you really scared Harry.' I grinned.

'That's one million per cent not true,' Harry shouted.

'Your aunt took a step back when she saw me too,' smiled Reema. 'She's so lovely, though. She helped carry my bag upstairs –' Reema was staying over – 'and said she'd

unpack for me, so I could join you right
away.'

'Aunt Nora's biscuits are delic–' began
Harry, then he pointed at the door and
burst out laughing. 'And who are *you*
supposed to be?'

Pongy – I mean, Oscar – had arrived.

'I'm *extremely* sorry,' he said in his high,
precise voice. 'But I do not possess any
masks. So, my mum suggested I dress up as
Doctor Who.' But all he had done was put

on a huge scarf and a bowler hat.

'You look more like Mr Benn,' said Harry.

Oscar's head drooped. 'I really didn't know what else to wear,' he muttered. 'I'm sorry. Have I spoiled everything?'

'Of course not!' cried Reema. 'Who cares about masks anyway?' And she immediately flung off her mask. 'We're just so happy you turned up – aren't we?'

'Why are you called Pongy?' Harry asked rudely.

I threw off my mask too and walked over to Oscar. 'Ignore my very annoying little brother. We do.'

'Little? I'm taller than you,' squealed Harry indignantly.

'And make yourself at home, even if the sofa is a bit lumpy.'

Shyly, awkwardly, Oscar perched himself between Reema and me.

'Time to tell bloodcurdling tales,' I announced.

I went first, followed by Reema, and then Harry. Finally, it was Oscar's turn. And do you know what, his story was the best. We all burst into applause at the end. Even Harry.

'And now time for those delicious-looking biscuits,' said Reema.

'Shame Harry's scoffed all his already.' I grinned.

The three of us sat on the sofa munching Aunt Nora's biscuits, while Harry whirled round and round on his chair. Oscar was even smiling a little now. I really thought he was starting to enjoy himself.

Suddenly, Oscar leapt to his feet.

'Aaaaargh!' he yelled. We all gaped in astonishment at him.

'Did you see that?' gasped Oscar.

'See what?' Reema and I demanded.

Oscar pointed a shaking hand at the window. 'I saw a face peering in at us.'

'It must have been Aunt Nora,' scoffed Harry.

'No, it wasn't,' cried Oscar. 'It was a werewolf.'

3

What Has Harry Done?

'A werewolf!? You must have imagined it,' I said at once, and Reema and I laughed nervously. Harry, very oddly, didn't say a single word.

'I tell you I saw a werewolf, and it was looking right at us.' Oscar was still standing up and his voice was shaking.

Suddenly, Reema and I leapt up too. We'd all heard the sound of . . . HOWLING.

WOOOOOOOOOOOOO!

'Wh–what's that then?' stuttered Oscar.

'What indeed?' I asked, turning to my brother. Harry was the only person still sitting down. And he couldn't stop a smile from creeping across his face either.

Of course – Harry had found my cape. And he'd wished for a werewolf. I knew it!

I gave him my very fiercest look. I was fuming. But I couldn't say anything with Oscar there. My magic cape was top secret.

Suddenly Oscar stopped shaking. Instead, he stared at Reema and me, his eyes full of suspicion. 'You don't seem very surprised there's a werewolf out there,' he said. 'And I know why. You've got some friends outside wearing masks and making spooky noises to try to frighten me.'

'We wouldn't do that to you,' said Reema. 'Honestly, we wouldn't.'

Oscar shook his head. 'I was so happy when you invited me round here tonight. But really you only wanted to make fun of me.'

That's when the howling began again, even louder this time.

Oscar stumbled towards the door. 'Well, now you can tell your friends how scared I got and have a good laugh, *can't* you?'

'No, don't go like this, Pongy . . .' I said.

Oscar whirled round and screamed, '*MY NAME IS OSCAR, NOT PONGY. AND I* HATE, HATE, HATE *BEING CALLED PONGY!*'

'I know – and I'm very, very sorry, I didn't mean to–' But Oscar had already pushed open the shed door. We saw him tear up the garden and rush out of the back gate.

Reema ran off after him. Only she skidded and slipped on the damp grass. I dived towards her.

'I'm all right,' gasped Reema, scrambling up and brushing bits of mud from her black clothes played a horrible trick on him . . .'

'I know,' I agreed, not knowing what else to say. We both walked dejectedly back to the shed.

'I can't help thinking I've made everything worse for Oscar,' said Reema. 'And I feel so awful.'

'It's not your fault,' I said, glaring at Harry, who was still swinging about in his chair.

'No, it's Jamie's fault for calling him Pongy,' said Harry.

'Never mind that,' I said. 'You used MY cape when I specifically asked you not to.'

'Well, you shouldn't have hidden it in such a stupidly easy place to find it,' said Harry.

'What?!' I exploded.

'So you wished for a werewolf?' Reema asked Harry.

'Yes, but only for tonight.' Harry grinned.

'And you must admit, it's made Halloween mega cool.'

'Not for Oscar,' snapped Reema.

'Yeah, well, I didn't know Oscar was coming,' said Harry. 'But if he had stayed a little longer, he would have seen a very small, very tame werewolf, with the most cheerful disposition. I wished especially for that.'

The howling sounds began again. 'It doesn't sound very cheerful,' I said.

'Or very small,' said Reema. Then she added urgently, 'Listen.'

'What?' I asked.

'I think it's right outside,' she hissed, 'trying to get in.'

'Don't worry,' I said. 'Harry's asked for a happy werewolf so it's probably just popping by for a glass of lemonade and to wish us a happy Halloween.'

'Well, I think it's horribly creepy,' said Reema, looking at Harry.

For the first time, Harry stopped smiling. In fact, he looked positively scared. But then he clambered out of his chair and said, 'Luckily I left this here earlier.' He dived down and held up his green slime shooter. 'I'll protect you from the werewolf and stop it pouncing on anyone,' he declared.

'Wait, Harry . . .' I began. But it was too late. He'd already charged outside.

'Take that!' he shouted at the dark shape right outside the door.

And then the shape spoke.

'Yeeeooow!' it shrieked.

4

Two Werewolves

'Stop attacking me,' the voice screeched on.

Reema and I gasped in horror. Green slime was dripping all the way down poor Oscar's face. It decorated his scarf and trousers too. Some had even splattered over his bowler hat.

Oscar was TOTALLY COVERED IN DISGUSTING GREEN GOO.

No wonder his legs were trembling as he

stumbled back inside the shed, with Harry dancing round him, still waving his shooter about.

'It was your fault. You shouldn't have been hiding outside,' protested Harry.

'I *wasn't* hiding,' Oscar spluttered. 'I was deciding if I'd been too hasty running off and should apologise.'

'It's so great you've come back,' I said.

'Yes it is,' cried Reema. 'Now, come and sit down, and we'll help you clean up.'

Oscar gave a large gulp as if he was about to burst into tears, but instead he sped away for the second time that evening.

'Oh no,' Reema said softly. 'Should I go after him?'

'Best leave it for now,' I said. 'Let him calm down.'

Then Harry began to shake with laughter. 'Oscar did look so funny,' he said.

'Shut up, Harry!' said Reema so fiercely – and she hardly ever gets angry – that he immediately stopped laughing.

Then we heard the werewolf howl again.

'I'll fetch my cape and just hope I can magic it away,' I said.

'Oh no, not yet!' cried Harry.

'What?' Reema and I shouted together.

'Well, it's made this Halloween so wicked,'

said Harry, 'knowing there's a werewolf outside.'

'No it hasn't,' I said.

'I wish you'd all stop worrying,' said Harry. 'I know for sure it's a tame, jolly werewolf, who only *sounds* dead spooky.'

'How do you know?' I asked.

'Because I've done something incredibly clever,' smirked Harry.

'Impossible,' I snapped.

'I know the cape's magic isn't very strong right now. So I had a brilliant idea. I made the same wish twice.'

'What?' I cried.

'Great! So there might be *two* werewolves lurking out there tonight,' said Reema, looking terrified.

'Don't be silly,' said Harry. 'I only asked

for one tame werewolf, but twice. And now I'll prove it's harmless.'

Harry dashed outside and yelled at the top of his voice, 'Hello, werewolf, did you know you've got stinky pants? And when you eat, you dribble. Ha ha.' Then he came back. 'See, nothing happened to me. The werewolf didn't leap out of the dark and bite my bottom.'

'What a shame,' I murmured. But Harry was extremely pleased with himself. 'I've made the magic cape work again!' He tore off his werewolf mask. 'That was getting so itchy,' he said. 'And I'm starving – can I finish off your biscuit, Reema?'

'No you can't . . .' she began and then stopped. Her eyes were like saucers. 'Look at Harry's face,' she whispered to me.

I stared at Harry.

And stared.

And stared some more.

Hair had started sprouting on Harry's chin. There were small tufts hanging under his nose and under his eyes too. Reema and I looked at each other in total horror.

HARRY WAS TURNING INTO A WEREWOLF.

'What's the matter?' he demanded. 'Why are you both looking at me with such silly expressions?' Harry's voice rose. 'Stop being silly . . .' He touched his chin, looking very puzzled. Then he ran his fingers all over his face. 'What's on my face?' he squeaked.

'It's hair,' I said quietly.

'But why?' asked Harry. 'What's happening to me?'

'You know my cape's magic is very weak right now. And it goes wrong sometimes.'

'Yes,' said Harry in an extremely small voice.

'Well, you wished for a werewolf twice – the first one is outside. And the other one . . .' I hesitated.

'Yes,' squeaked Harry.

'Well . . . by mistake, I think the cape is turning you into a werewolf too.'

Harry screeched in horror and sprang up. Then he pulled off his werewolf claws and screeched again. Hair was growing over his hands.

'But I don't want to be a werewolf,' he wailed.

Then I noticed something else. Harry's teeth were turning all sharp and pointy as well. And more hair was creeping over his face. How long before he turned into a werewolf completely?

'I can't go to school looking like this tomorrow!' Harry was very close to tears now.

'But that would be AMAZING!' I said. 'The whole school would go mad when they saw you. Then they'd ring up the zoo.'

'The *zoo*,' yelled Harry. 'I can't live in a zoo!'

'Don't worry, we'll come and visit you,' I said. 'Now and again.'

'Oh, Jamie, help me,' cried Harry. Big fat tears were rushing down his face now. 'Change me back, please.'

Harry didn't often ask me for help. He

must have been really, really worried. That's why I said, 'All right, I'll go and get my cape right now.'

'Thanks,' he said. Then he gave a little shriek as more hair sprouted up on his hands. 'Hurry up, Jamie,' he urged.

'Don't worry, we'll sort everything out.' Reema put a comforting arm round my werewolf brother.

'Be back very soon . . .' I began, then froze.

Someone was knocking on the door. The three of us looked at each other in alarm.

'I can't let anyone see me like this,' hissed Harry.

'Do you think it's Oscar?' I asked.

'I don't think he'd come back a second time,' Reema replied.

'Well, maybe it's the werewolf looking for

a friend,' I joked. But neither Reema nor Harry smiled.

'Just stay quiet and they might go away,' whispered Harry.

But then a high, sweet voice wafted through the door. 'Come on, children, open the door. I'm carrying a tray of hot chocolate for you all.'

It was Aunt Nora.

What were we going to do?

5

Werewolf Brother

We had to think fast.

'I'll switch the lights off,' said Reema.

'Good idea,' I said. 'And, Harry, sit very still.'

That's when Harry made a very strange noise. 'Parp! Parp!' he said.

'Harry, this is no time to act silly,' I snapped.

'Parp! Parp!' he said again. 'Sorry, but I

just can't stop myself. It's exactly like when you have hiccups. They jump out of you. Parp . . . parp!'

'It's like a tiny growl,' said Reema. 'The kind a baby werewolf might make.'

'It sounds more like a tiny fart to me,' I said. We all giggled.

'Look, Harry, just hold your breath or something – only try to stop parping.'

I opened the door to a beaming Aunt Nora. 'Hello, dears, are you having a

wonderful time?' She peered around. 'But it's so dark in here.'

'Adds to the atmosphere, Aunt Nora,' I said.

'Well, I've made you all a nice cup of hot chocolate.' Aunt Nora was a great believer in hot chocolate, especially at night. 'And there's one of my home-made biscuits for each of you as well.'

'That's terrific.' I took the tray from her and put it down on the table, which I could just about see. 'Well, thanks so much for dropping by,' I added, hoping she'd take the hint and leave.

Instead, Aunt Nora went on squinting around her. 'But where's your friend?' she asked.

'Oscar had to go home,' I said.

'Oh, what a shame,' she sighed. 'He seemed such a nice boy too.'

'Yes, he is very, very nice,' said Reema, shaking her head sadly. I knew she was still upset about Oscar thinking we'd wanted to make fun of him.

'Well, even though it's Halloween, I'm still going to be a bit strict about bedtime,' Aunt Nora told us. 'It's a school day tomorrow, you know. So I want you all back inside in just ten minutes.'

'Parp . . . parp, parp.' The sounds erupted from the back of the room.

'Harry, that's very rude,' said Aunt Nora. 'I know you'd like to stay here longer, but you're already up past your bedtime.'

'Parp, parp, parp,' cried Harry.

'I think someone has forgotten their

manners,' said Aunt Nora.

'Sorry,' said Harry, but then two more 'parps' burst out of him.

'He's very excited,' I said.

Harry gave his loudest 'parp' yet in reply. But I'd already taken Aunt Nora's hand and was guiding her firmly outside.

The full moon had now gone behind the clouds. I heard a rustling sound. Then a twig crackled. Was that the werewolf we'd heard earlier, skulking about? And was he really the friendly, tame werewolf that Harry had wished for?

I left Aunt Nora in the kitchen and raced upstairs. I opened the case, flung my smelly socks and old comics on the floor and seized my cape. But then I jumped back with horror. For one awful moment

I thought the once wonderfully bright gold stars around the side of my cape had completely vanished.

But no, they were still there – only so faint you had to stare really hard to find them. No wonder I had a huge lump in my throat. My wonderful, dazzling, brilliant cape seemed to be disappearing before my eyes. And was all the magic leaking out of it too?

This was Harry's fault. I'd told him the cape needed a rest to let the magic soak back in to it. But he wouldn't listen – as usual. And it's not *his* cape. IT'S MINE. He had no business even breathing on it. So it would serve him right. Let him turn into my werewolf brother. I'd enjoy watching Harry become hairier than a gorilla.

But deep down – very, very deep down – I knew I couldn't let that happen. And that I'd do my very best to change Harry back. And get rid of that werewolf in the garden.

So I picked up a little bottle of water, as well as my cape, and bounded downstairs.

'Bye, Aunt Nora,' I shouted.

'Hope your hot chocolate isn't cold now,' she called after me. 'And, Jamie …' I sprang round. 'Keep an eye on Harry for me, will you? I'm a little bit worried about him.'

I was VERY worried about him.

Back at the shed, Harry was jumping about as if he had a wasp in his pants.

'If I move about a lot it stops me parping so much,' he gasped. 'I hate being a werewolf. Please get a move on, Jamie. I just feel so itchy … everywhere.'

'All right, keep your fur on,' I muttered. I squirted water all over the cape, then wished out loud . . . 'Magic cape, please change Harry back to his old, very annoying self and make the werewolf outside vanish.'

'And do it now,' prompted Harry.

'And please do it now,' I said.

I opened my eyes. With a heavy, sinking feeling I saw Harry was just as hairy as before . . .

Outside in the garden the werewolf howled, as if to remind us it was still there too.

'I was afraid this might happen,' I said. 'There's hardly any magic left in my cape. And certainly not enough to break two spells.'

'Maybe,' suggested Reema, 'if we all wish together, it might help the magic grow stronger.'

So this time we all held on to the still very wet cape. And I suggested we close our eyes too, so we could really concentrate on our wish.

Finally, we opened our eyes. I hardly dared to even look. Harry let out a very loud groan. 'NOTHING'S HAPPENED – AGAIN! And it's all the cape's fault.'

'But something *has* changed,' Reema said unexpectedly. 'Harry's not getting any hairier.'

I studied him for a moment.

'You're right, he's not,' I cried excitedly. 'And he's stopped making that stupid noise as well.'

'So you're only a bit of a werewolf now, Harry,' said Reema brightly.

'But I don't want to be a bit of a werewolf,' wailed Harry. 'I want to be all me again.'

Then we heard Aunt Nora calling us. 'Time for bed, children. Hurry up and come inside, please.'

Harry folded his arms. 'Well, I'm not going anywhere,' he said stubbornly.

6

Big Trouble

'You can't stay here all night, Harry,' said Reema.

'Oh yes I can.' Harry plonked himself down again on the swing chair.

'So, what will I tell Aunt Nora?' I asked.

'Tell her . . .' Harry considered. 'Tell her I've run away . . . to live on the moon.'

I glared at Harry. 'If you don't come with us now, do you know what I'll do?'

'No.' Harry looked at me very warily.

'I will wish all night on my cape, for you to be turned into the world's smelliest toad. You're dead stinky already, so it shouldn't take too much magic.'

'You wouldn't.' Harry's eyes were nearly popping out of his head.

'Oh yes I would,' I said.

'And you'll be so much more comfortable in your own warm bed,' said Reema.

Harry stopped swinging around. 'All right, I'll come with you. But only because I don't want to worry Aunt Nora.'

'In that case,' I said, 'keep your head down, so she doesn't see your hairy face. And keep your hands behind your back, so she doesn't spot your sprouting fur. And most of all, Aunt Nora mustn't catch sight of your monster teeth. So don't open your mouth. That is VERY IMPORTANT.'

'Why don't you just put a sheet over me?' said Harry.

'That would be a definite improvement,' I snapped.

We walked quickly up the garden, me carrying the tray of mugs. 'As soon as we go inside,' I whispered to Harry, 'you leg it . . . We'll say you're very, very sleepy.'

Harry raced into the kitchen with his hands behind his back, looking as if he was about to do some Irish dancing.

Unfortunately, he hadn't thought Aunt Nora would be waiting for us just inside the door. And he was running so fast he NEARLY collided with her.

'Harry, why are you rushing about like

that?' demanded Aunt Nora.

'Well, Aunt Nora,' Harry said, 'we didn't want to let you down and be late.'

Aunt Nora turned pink with pleasure. 'What a lovely thing to say.' She smiled at us.

'You're feeling very tired, aren't you, Harry?' I began.

But I was too late. Aunt Nora had glimpsed his face and immediately shrieked, 'Harry!'

'I know, he's ugly, isn't he?' I said.

'What on earth have you put on your face?' gasped Aunt Nora.

At least Harry remembered not to open his mouth very much. Instead, sounding like someone who has just been to the dentist to have twenty teeth out, he mumbled something no one could understand.

Aunt Nora was looking more and more

bewildered.

'I think Harry got a bit frightened tonight,' said Reema.

'The poor lamb. I expect that's why he was making all those silly noises earlier.'

And suddenly Aunt Nora was staring very sternly – at me! 'Jamie, I expected you to look after your brother – not stick hair on his face and scare the poor boy so much he can't even speak properly.'

'But, Aunt Nora–' I began.

'You will go upstairs with your brother, Jamie, and help him clean his face, please.'

Harry and I bounded upstairs to his bedroom. 'When am I going to stop being a werewolf?' Harry's voice was actually shaking.

'Soon . . . I hope.' I squirted more water on my cape. I closed my eyes and wished so hard I went red in the face and felt quite dizzy.

But it was no good.

Then I had an idea. 'Why don't I borrow

Dad's razor, then you can–'
'I'm too young to shave!' wailed Harry.

'Shh,' I snapped. 'Aunt Nora is only next door.'
I was sure Reema was asking Aunt Nora lots of questions, to give me more time to turn Harry back. But what else could I do?

'Harry, please, just have a little shave,' I pleaded.

'No.' He shook his head, making the hair on his chin flutter about. 'Instead I'm going to tell Aunt Nora all about the magic cape.'

'You wouldn't,' I gasped. 'You *couldn't*. The cape is TOP SECRET.'

'And I'll tell her how you put me under a spell, which means I've got to stay a werewolf for ever!'

'Excuse me, Harry,' I hissed. 'YOU did that ... Anyway, there's no point in panicking because ...' I paused.

'Go on,' said Harry.

'Well, things can't get any worse,' I said.

'Now, how are we getting on?' came a voice from the door.

Yes they could.

Aunt Nora was actually inside Harry's bedroom! No wonder shivers ran up and down my spine and my brain just froze. How could I explain my hairy brother?

And what would Aunt Nora do?

Ring my parents? Definitely. They would go completely bananas. And you couldn't blame them! 'Just to let you know, your son's a werewolf now. Bye.'

Aunt Nora clapped her hands. What on earth was she going to say?

'Now, boys, that's much better.' She smiled. 'You have cleaned yourself up so nicely, Harry. Well done.'

I slowly looked at my brother. It couldn't be true, could it?

But, yes, at the very last millisecond the cape must have finally worked its magic.

And not only had all the signs of being a werewolf left Harry, but his face was positively glowing. And his teeth had never shone whiter. You know how cups and plates sparkle when they're brought out of the dishwasher? Well, that's exactly how Harry looked. I thought I'd burst with relief.

'That's better,' trilled Aunt Nora. 'But we're rather late so, Harry, dear, pop straight into your pyjamas and soon you'll be faraway in the land of Nod. I'll just get Reema that extra blanket.'

She bustled out and I said, 'Phew! The cape came through in the end.' I walked to the door. 'Glad that's all over.'

'Um . . . not quite,' smiled Harry. 'You see, I actually made *three* wishes.'

I gulped. 'Three?!'

'Yes, I thought we might feel a bit sad after Halloween finished, so I made a third wish for tomorrow night.'

'What is it?' I demanded at once.

'The most brilliant, amazing, incredible wish,' said Harry, a big smile on his face.

'What is it? Tell me . . .'

'That's for me to know and for you to find out.' Harry kept on grinning.

'You really are the most annoying brother in the whole universe,' I shouted. I couldn't bear to hear any more. I shot into my bedroom, where one question raced round and round in my head.

What on earth was Harry's third wish?

7

Operation Oscar

The next morning Harry still wouldn't tell me anything about his third wish. And you should have seen the way Aunt Nora fussed over him at breakfast. I nearly threw up.

In the end Reema and I left early for school. I tried to tell her about Harry's extra wish, but she was far too worried about Oscar to pay any attention.

'I was the only person at school he trusted,' she said. 'And now he thinks I've let him down.'

We spotted Oscar on the playground, on his own as usual. We sped over to him.

'Hi, Oscar …' began Reema, but he walked away from us.

'Oscar, just hear us out,' she began.

'No, leave me alone,' he cried, speeding up into a run.

Reema stood staring hard at the trees on the school's back field. I knew she was trying to stop herself from crying. 'What are we going to do?' she said at last.

'We'll keep on trying to talk to him,' I replied.

And we did.

We tried at the start of morning lessons

and at break time. But both times he just turned away. A boy even called across to us. 'Why do you want to talk to Pongy?'

'Because we really like him,' I called back. I think Oscar might have heard me say that. I really hoped he had.

Then at the end of the morning, Oscar was trudging his way to the dining hall when I yelled, 'Oscar, how would you like to squirt slime at me?'

The question surprised him so much he actually stopped walking.

'I'll lend you Harry's slime shooter tonight and you can squirt it all over me, if you want,' I went on.

'Me as well,' said Reema.

Oscar slowly turned round, and stood frowning at us . . .

'Last night really was an accident,' said Reema.

Oscar didn't say anything, but at least he wasn't running away from us.

'I used to have a nickname,' I said. 'A few boys called me the Shrimp and they laughed every time they said it.' I shuddered.

'That's nearly as bad as being called Pongy,' said Oscar.

'Worse.' I grinned and then said to him, 'Why don't we do another Halloween in my shed tonight, just the three of us this time. And if you don't enjoy yourself—'

'I get to cover you in green slime?' interrupted Oscar.

'Exactly. Now, how amazing is that for an offer?' I asked.

Oscar just went on frowning.

'Go on, say yes,' urged Reema. 'You won't be sorry.'

'And think of Reema and me, dripping goo everywhere,' I said.

A reluctant smile crept across Oscar's face.

'Please come,' begged Reema.

Oscar considered it for another moment. Then he said shyly, 'Shall I turn up at the same time as last night?'

'Perfect,' said Reema. She was smiling.

Everyone was smiling. I felt so happy — until the end of school.

I was on my own, as Reema had to go to the dentist for an emergency filling. To my surprise, I saw that Harry was waiting for me. We hardly ever talk at school and we never, *ever* walk home together. Yet there he was. I was not pleased to see him.

But then he said in a trembling voice, 'Jamie, look at my hands.'

I glanced down at them quickly — they were covered in mud as usual. But something was different. On the back of each one were a few strands of black frizzy hair.

WEREWOLF HAIR.

And underneath his nose there was the beginnings of a moustache. You had to look closely to spot it. But it was there all right.

'How long–' I began.

'Only since the last lesson,' interrupted Harry. 'It was just starting to get dark when I felt this tickling on my hand. As it gets darker, do you think I'll grow more and more hairy again?' Panic filled his face.

'Maybe it's to do with your third wish,' I suggested.

'But that had nothing to do with werewolves,' cried Harry. 'I'm *sick* of werewolves. And I know what you're going to say – I should never have wished on your cape in the first place. I was stupid. I admit it.'

'Wow, that's a first,' I said.

'But what are we going to do now?' cried Harry.

'The magic in the cape is still very weak,'

I explained. 'So, it managed to temporarily break the spell last night, but it isn't strong enough to stop the werewolf creeping back when it gets dark again.'

Harry suddenly opened his mouth very wide. 'What about my teeth? Have they changed? Have a look.'

I took a look. A couple of girls watching us giggled and one asked me, 'What are you doing, Jamie? Checking Harry's cleaned his teeth today?'

'The teeth haven't changed at all,' I muttered, feeling very embarrassed. 'Now close your mouth and let's go home – fast.'

'Hello, boys, looking forward to the weekend?' Aunt Nora welcomed us home.

'We sure are,' I said.

Aunt Nora looked at Harry. He'd remembered to keep his head down and his arms behind his back. 'Are you all right, dear?' she asked.

'Oh yes, I'm very happy,' said Harry in the most miserable voice ever.

Then we bounded upstairs. I wished and wished on my cape, but the hairs stayed on Harry's face and hands. 'At least you're not getting any hairier,' I said.

'Not yet,' said Harry gloomily. 'You wait until it really gets dark.'

Aunt Nora hadn't noticed anything odd about Harry's appearance – yet – but I had to keep him out of her way. So I persuaded her to let Harry and me have our tea in the Halloween hideaway.

We took over sandwiches and slices of Aunt Nora's home-made cake and fresh fruit for afters. Turning into a werewolf certainly hadn't taken away Harry's appetite. Although every so often he would yell out, 'Ow,' as another hair appeared on his face or hands.

I was taking our plates back to the kitchen when Reema arrived. I had just started to tell her about Harry when a great roar from the garden filled the air.

Reema and I shuddered. 'So the other werewolf's back too,' I hissed. 'I've got my cape and a little bottle of water,' I said. 'So all I can do is keep wishing.'

'What about Oscar?' cried Reema suddenly. 'He's on his way here and if he hears that werewolf again–'

'He will think we're trying to scare him,' I interrupted.

'And he'll never ever trust us again,' said Reema anxiously. 'Jamie, what are we going to do?'

'I know, I'll ring and tell him I've got a nasty tummy bug. I'm throwing up everywhere . . . so it would be better if he came round another night.'

Reema sighed heavily. 'I think that's for the best. Poor Oscar.'

Then the doorbell rang. And we heard Aunt Nora say, 'Come in, dear. Lovely to see you again – I do hope you can stay a little longer tonight. Reema and Jamie are just in the kitchen.'

'Too late,' murmured Reema.

And there was Oscar.

Seeing our startled faces he said, 'Oh, I'm sorry. I'm a bit early, aren't I?'

'No, no,' Reema and I chorused. 'It's brilliant to see you.'

Oscar grinned. 'I am so looking forward to tonight.'

8

The Werewolf in the Garden

Five minutes later, Reema, Oscar and I were in the shed, sitting on the lumpy sofa. Reema had brought over some big, plump cushions to try to make it more comfortable. Meanwhile, Harry was once again reclining on the black chair – only this time he wasn't swinging about at all.

'Harry,' Reema called across to him, 'I think you've got something to say to Oscar, haven't you?'

'Have I?' he began. 'Oh yes, I'm very, very sorry for mistaking you for a werewolf – and for covering you in slime. To make up for it you can call me Farty Face, if you want.'

Oscar smiled. But then his smile froze.

'Listen,' he whispered.

The howling was definitely louder tonight. It rumbled on for longer too, sounding a bit like thunder . . . I so wished it *were* thunder.

'Your werewolf is back,' said Oscar, when the howling had finished.

'It's not *our* werewolf,' Reema said quickly.

'We really don't know what it is,' I said. That was true. It sounded like a werewolf but it could be *anything* out there – mysterious and menacing.

'Well, whatever it is, it's in your garden again,' said Oscar in a low, flat voice.

'It does sound especially close tonight,' Reema agreed.

Under my breath I kept whispering to my cape, 'Make that werewolf vanish and stop my brother transforming into one, PLEASE.' I was certain my cape was really trying to help, but its magic was so faint that it couldn't quite manage it.

Oscar jumped up.

'Please don't go.' Reema leapt to her feet too.

'I'm not leaving,' said Oscar. 'I'm going to see this werewolf.'

'What?' I exclaimed. 'You can't just go waltzing off after werewolves.'

'Why not?' said Oscar, opening the shed door and striding outside.

We tore after him.

'Oscar, be careful,' cried Reema.

The moon looked huge and hung over the garden. The sky was crowded with tiny silver stars gazing down on us.

'I think the werewolf is over there,' Oscar whispered. He pointed towards the large trees, right at the end of the garden. The trees seemed to be whispering to each other in the light gentle breeze. And the branches cast shadows like very long fingers over the leaves on the ground.

'Yes, I see it!' cried Oscar. 'There's something crouched under the tree right in front of us.'

Harry's hairy hand squeezed mine, the fur tickling my hand. Reema was standing very close to me too. And then we all saw a pair of purple eyes glinting in the moonlight.

WEREWOLF EYES.

'Children, what on earth are you doing in the garden?' cried a voice.

It was Aunt Nora, calling from the patio.

'We're just showing Oscar our trees,' I shouted back.

Reema giggled. So did Harry. It sounded like such a weird thing to be doing. But it was all I could think of.

'They are splendid trees,' Aunt Nora called back. 'But you will see them much better in daylight. And don't get cold out there, will you?'

'Don't worry, we won't,' I said.

'We'll just get eaten by a werewolf instead,' joked Harry.

'Well done in finding the werewolf, Oscar,' said Reema. 'But I think we should go back inside the shed now.'

'I agree,' said Harry, squeezing my hand even tighter.

Oscar turned round for a moment, the breeze ruffling his hair. 'You go back if you like, but I'm going to see this werewolf properly.'

'What?' shrieked Harry.

Oscar began walking forward. 'Werewolf,' he hissed. 'Come on out, show yourself.'

And that's when the werewolf moved.

9

Oscar Is Very Brave

'Don't get too close to it, Oscar!' I shouted warningly. At the same time I held on to my cape, dropped some water on it, and made another wish. 'Just make that werewolf disappear – for all our sakes,' I pleaded, and the cape actually twitched, as if to say it was trying its hardest.

But it was no good.

The werewolf was still there. In my garden.

And now I saw it slowly shuffling towards Oscar, its claws brushing the ground . . .

'It really is a teenie-weenie one,' whispered Harry. 'Exactly as I wished for.'

In fact, it was about the size of an Alsatian puppy and looked very similar to a dog. Only this werewolf had large, very hairy ears and its whole body was covered in thick black fur. It also had large purple eyes.

Then it stopped moving and let out a low howl, and we could see how sharp and pointed its teeth were too. But Oscar went on whispering to the werewolf to come closer to him.

'He's amazingly brave,' Reema whispered to me.

'What's he saying to the werewolf?' asked Harry.

I strained to listen. Oscar was talking very quietly, but I could just hear what he was saying: 'Don't worry, don't be afraid. Honestly, you can trust me.'

Then something happened that I never expected. As the werewolf drew closer to him, Oscar stretched out his hand and started patting its fur, just as if it were a pet. OSCAR'S PET WEREWOLF.

The werewolf not only let him, but gave these happy, contented little whines, sounding exactly like a lost puppy reunited with its owner.

And then the werewolf disappeared.

One moment it was there ... the very next, it had vanished. And Oscar was patting the air. No wonder he jumped back.

Harry let out a delighted yelp. 'All the hair on my hands and face has vanished,' he cried.

And it really had.

Oscar's bravery must have helped my cape finally break the spell.

The three of us sped over to him. 'Let me shake you by the hand, Oscar,' I said to him.

'You were completely awesome,' said Reema.

'You can have my slime shooter to keep forever, if you like,' said Harry.

Oscar was looking totally bewildered. 'I can't believe I did it,' he gulped.

I put an arm round Oscar's shoulders. 'Let's go back to the shed.'

There, he explained. 'When I heard that werewolf howling, I knew it was miserable and lonely.'

'How did you know that?' asked Reema.

'I just did,' said Oscar. 'That's why I wasn't really scared. I thought he was unhappy and wanted a friend.'

'And you were so right,' I said.

'But when I patted it . . .' began Oscar.

'Still can't believe you did that,' said Harry.

'My hand just went right through it,' continued Oscar. 'As if it was only a werewolf in a dream. So no one will ever believe us, if we try to tell them about tonight.'

'It's our secret then,' I said.

Then Oscar admitted how he had never wanted to move here. 'I missed all my old friends so much. And I was really nervous on my first day. Then when I said "pongy" . . .'

'Everyone started calling you that and never gave you a chance,' finished Reema.

'But you've made some new friends now,' I said.

'Three new friends,' said Harry. 'Well, four if you count the werewolf.'

Just then, Aunt Nora came in with our hot chocolate. 'Have you enjoyed yourself tonight, dear?' she asked Oscar.

'Oh yes,' replied Oscar, his eyes shining. 'I've had the best time ever.'

After Oscar had gone home, the three of us were left in the kitchen.

'It's been fun, but I'm so glad it's all over now,' said Reema.

'Oh, but it isn't,' declared Harry. 'You're forgetting my third wish.'

10

The Midnight Visitor

'Come on, Harry. You've got to tell us now. What have you wished for?' I said.

'If I told you, it wouldn't be a surprise.' Harry grinned. 'But you will really, *really* like it.'

'Except the magic's incredibly weak right now,' I pointed out. 'So your wish could easily go a bit wrong.'

'Don't worry, I've thought of that,' said

Harry, puffing out his chest. He was so pleased with himself; it was so annoying.

'That's why I wished for my guest to appear in our back garden at midnight, which is the most magic time anyway, making it much easier for my wish to come true. I really am super clever.'

'No, you're a numpty head,' I replied.

Reema giggled.

'What did you just call me?' demanded Harry.

'Bedtime, dears,' announced Aunt Nora. 'Come on, I'm sure you're very tired and looking forward to a good night's sleep.'

We all smiled at Aunt Nora. If only she knew. I set my alarm for quarter to twelve and found a clock for Reema – Harry said he wouldn't need one as he would be unable to sleep a wink because he was far too excited.

The plan was we'd all creep downstairs and wait for Harry's 'guest' on the patio. I would have my cape with me just in case the midnight visitor wasn't exactly who Harry was expecting. Anything could happen tonight.

To my surprise, I fell asleep almost at once. Aunt Nora was right; I was very tired. And when my alarm went off it took me a few seconds to work out what the sound was. I quickly sprang out of bed and had just bunged on my dressing gown when Reema tapped lightly on my door.

We set off to get Harry. He was snoring his head off as usual, fast asleep.

I shook him and he still didn't wake up.

I shook him much harder.

'Stop that! Stop that now!' he yelled.

'Shh, keep your voice down,' I said.

'Well, don't push me like that,' he cried. 'I nearly had an accident in my pants.'

'We'll just let you carry on sleeping then,' I said.

Harry dived out of his bed so fast he slammed right into his wardrobe.

'Will you be quiet?' I hissed. 'Aunt Nora's only a little bit deaf.'

'Don't tell me what to do,' grumbled Harry. 'This is my wish, not yours!'

'And it's *my* cape,' I reminded him for the one millionth time.

We all tiptoed downstairs, threw on our coats and very carefully opened the patio door.

Outside, the garden was bathed in moonlight, and everything was sunk in a thick silence. It was so quiet we could hear a clock striking midnight somewhere in the distance. I gave a shiver of anticipation. Harry started counting down. 'Eight, seven, six, five . . .'

Then we all joined in. 'Four, three, two, one . . .'

MIDNIGHT.

Bong! Bong! Bong!

Reema let out a gasp, while Harry stood as still as a statue.

Something was in the garden.

11

The Werecorn

It stood, right at the end of the garden, in a bright patch of moonlight.

A white horse.

The tallest white horse I had ever seen.

Suddenly I noticed something else – an odd little silver horn sticking right out of its forehead.

'It's a unicorn,' gasped Reema. 'Is that what you wished for, Harry?'

Harry looked petrified. He just kept on gazing at it.

The unicorn was a gleaming, milky-white colour, yet its tail and hooves were silver.

'It's so beautiful,' said Reema. 'A real unicorn. I think I'll explode with happiness!'

I knew exactly what Reema meant.

'Hey, unicorn!' shouted Harry suddenly. 'You're brilliant and awesome and—'

'Keep your voice down,' I urged.

The unicorn's sky-blue eyes fixed on us for a moment. Then it drew back its curled neck and let out the strangest sound I'd ever heard – half a neigh and half a howl. At the same time we saw its teeth: they were sharp and pointed. A werewolf's teeth.

'It's a unicorn,' whispered Reema. 'But also a bit of a werewolf.'

'A werecorn,' I said.

The werecorn raised one of its silver hooves.

'Is it about to charge at us?' cried Harry.

'No, idiot, it's saying goodbye to us,' I said. And it was.

'Oh, it's gone already,' said Reema. And we stood there, blinking, like at the end of a brilliant firework display.

'How wicked was that?' said Harry. He turned towards me. 'What did you call it?'

'A werecorn.'

'So we've seen the only werecorn in the entire world,' said Harry. 'Thanks to me.'

'All right, Mr Smarty-pants,' I began. But then I stopped. I couldn't believe what I'd just noticed. It was totally fantastic.

I let Harry tumble, yawning, into the kitchen.

'Quick,' I hissed to Reema, 'before we go inside – take a look at my cape.'

She stared at it and her whole face lit up. 'Oh, Jamie, all the stars are shining again.'

'And look at the seven,' I said. 'It's glowing away now.'

'Unicorns are supposed to be the most magical creatures of all. So maybe this werecorn helped the magic rush back into your cape?' said Reema.

'I think you're right, and it's totally amazing to see my cape looking like its old self again.' I lowered my voice, 'Now, not a word to Harry.'

'Not a word to me about what?' Harry's face popped out again.

'Nothing . . .' I began.

'Do you mean about the magic coming back to the cape?' he said.

'You were eavesdropping!' I cried.

'Of course I was.' Harry grinned at me. 'We're going to have some epic fun now, aren't we?'

Reema and I couldn't help smiling too.

'You know what, Harry,' I said. 'We really are.'

Look out for more

A JAMIE'S
AMAZING
CAPE ADVENTURE

HAVE YOU
READ THEM ALL?

BUG BROTHER

Jamie finds a cape covered in gold stars.
He likes to pretend it grants wishes.

One day, Jamie's little brother Harry is
really bugging him and Jamie makes a wish
that Harry will turn into a bluebottle.

But this is no ordinary cape
and soon Jamie is plunged into
a magical adventure . . .

ISBN: 9781846471001

PIRATE BROTHER

Jamie has the perfect wish for his
magic cape – to hang out with Brave Bill,
the magic pirate from his favourite book!

But then Jamie's little brother steals his wish!
Harry is off sailing the seven seas and Jamie
is miserable – until Brave Bill turns
up in Jamie's bedroom.

Jamie takes Bill to class, but magic
pirate + school = disaster and it's
up to him to save the day!

ISBN: 9781846470875

INVISIBLE BROTHER

Jamie is sick of his little brother Harry
showing off all the time. If only
Harry would disappear!

But then Harry makes a wish on Jamie's
amazing magic cloak and hey presto –
he's invisible!

Now it's up to Jamie to turn him back . . .

ISBN: 9781846471018

DETECTIVE BROTHER

Jamie and Harry are meant to be on
holiday at the seaside, but when Mrs. Jones's
sparkly earrings get stolen, Jamie finds
he is the number-one suspect.

To make things worse, his magic cape
seems to have lost its powers . . .

Will Jamie's cape help him
find the real villain?

ISBN: 9781846471179

PETE
JOHNSON

Pete Johnson has been a film extra, a film critic for Radio One, an English teacher and a journalist. However, his dream was always to be a writer. At the age of ten he wrote a fan letter to Dodie Smith, author of *The Hundred and One Dalmatians*, and they wrote to each other for many years. Dodie Smith was the first person to encourage him to be a writer.

Pete is a best-selling author for children and teenagers whose books have been translated into over twenty languages. In 2009 he won The Sheffield Community Award.

www.petejohnsonauthor.com